Another Sommer-Time Story™

You Move You Lose

By Carl Sommer
Illustrated by Kennon James

Advance • HOUSTON
PUBLSHING, INC.

Permissions
Advance Publishing, Inc.
6950 Fulton St.
Houston, TX 77022

www.advancepublishing.com

First Edition
Printed in Singapore

Library of Congress Cataloging-in-Publication Data

Sommer, Carl, 1930-
   You Move, You Lose / by Carl Sommer; illustrated by Kennon James. -- 1st ed.
      p. cm. -- (Another Sommer-Time Story)
   Summary: Prissy and Stubby Bear are so stubborn that their forest friends decide to teach them a lesson they'll never forget.
   Cover Title: Carl Sommer's You Move, You Lose.
ISBN 1-57537-005-0 (hardcover: alk. paper). -- ISBN 1-57537-056-5 (library binding: alk. paper)
   [1. Obstinacy Fiction. 2. Bears Fiction. 3. Brothers and sisters Fiction.] I. James, Kennon, ill. II. Title. III. Title: Carl Sommer's You Move, You Lose. IV. Series: Sommer, Carl, 1930- Another Sommer-Time Story.
PZ7.S696235Yo 2000   99-35283
[E]--dc21   CIP

You Move You Lose

Once there was a young cub named Stubby. Bucky Beaver thought Stubby was the most stubborn bear in the forest.

Ricky Rabbit disagreed. He thought Prissy, Stubby's sister, was the most stubborn bear.

Papa and Mama taught their cubs about sharing and being kind to one another, but Stubby and Prissy would not listen.

Stubby always wanted to have *his* way, and Prissy always wanted to have *her* way—or else there was trouble.

When their forest friends came over to play, Stubby and Prissy would always end up fussing and yelling at each other.

"Why are you cubs so stubborn?" Daisy Deer would ask. "We can't have fun when you act that way."

But Stubby and Prissy would never listen. So everyone would stop playing and go home.

One day Mama said, "Papa and I are going outside to pick berries and nuts."

"If you need us," added Papa, "just call us. We'll be nearby."

"Now be kind to each other while we're gone," said Mama.

"Okay," said Stubby and Prissy.

Papa picked up a big box. As he left the house, he said, "Would someone please close the door after us?"

"Prissy," said Stubby, "go and shut the door."

"Why should I?" asked Prissy. "You're the closest. Why don't *you* shut the door?"

Before they could decide on who should shut the door, their forest friends came by.

"Stubby! Prissy!" called Bucky Beaver.

"Come on in!" yelled Prissy. "We're playing a game."

"Great!" shouted Ricky Rabbit. "We want to play too."

As everyone sat around the table, a blast of cold air blew through the open door.

"Brrrrrr, I'm cold," said Prissy.

"So am I," said Ricky Rabbit.

"Prissy," said Stubby, "since you're now the closest to the door, why don't you shut it?"

"Why should *I* shut the door?" complained Prissy. "You were closest to the door when Papa asked *you* to shut it."

"Papa didn't ask *me* to close the door," Stubby snapped back. "He asked if *someone* would close the door. *Someone* could be you. Don't be lazy. You're the closest now, so go and shut the door!"

"Don't tell me what to do, Stubby," growled Prissy. "And don't call me lazy!"

"You *are* lazy—and stubborn!" yelled Stubby.

"I'm not lazy!" Prissy yelled back. "And I'm not stubborn! *You're* lazy, and *you're* stubborn—and mean!"

"Oh, nooooo!" groaned Daisy Deer. "Here they
go again—fussing, yelling, and being stubborn."

Quietly their forest friends left the house.

"Look!" growled Stubby. "Our friends have
left just because *you* wouldn't close the door!"

"Well," snapped Prissy, "if *you* had obeyed
Papa, we'd still be playing!"

Prissy could think of nothing else to say, and neither could Stubby. They climbed up onto the couch and stared at each other. Suddenly, Prissy got an idea.

"I'll make a deal with you," she said. "Since

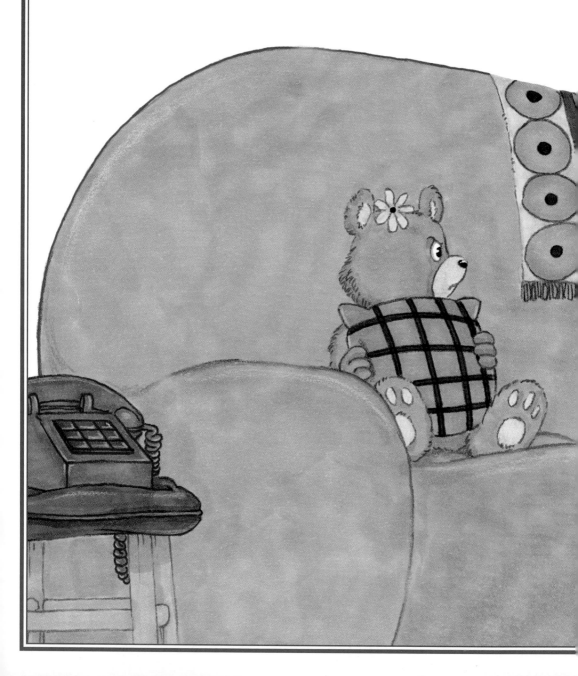

we don't want to talk anymore, and we don't want to shut the door, let's have a contest. The first one who talks, closes the door."

"Better yet," challenged Stubby, "the first one who talks or *moves,* closes the door."

"Okay!" snapped Prissy. "You move, you lose!"

Stubby pointed his finger and growled, "It's a deal! You move, you lose!"

Stubby and Prissy made themselves comfortable. Stubby folded his arms, and Prissy grabbed a pillow.

Then they sat and stared at each other. No one moved or made a sound.

"Is he ever hard-headed," thought Prissy. "But I'll teach him a lesson he'll never forget!"

As Stubby stared at Prissy, he thought, "For a bear, she sure is proud and stubborn. But I'll show her. I'll never give in!"

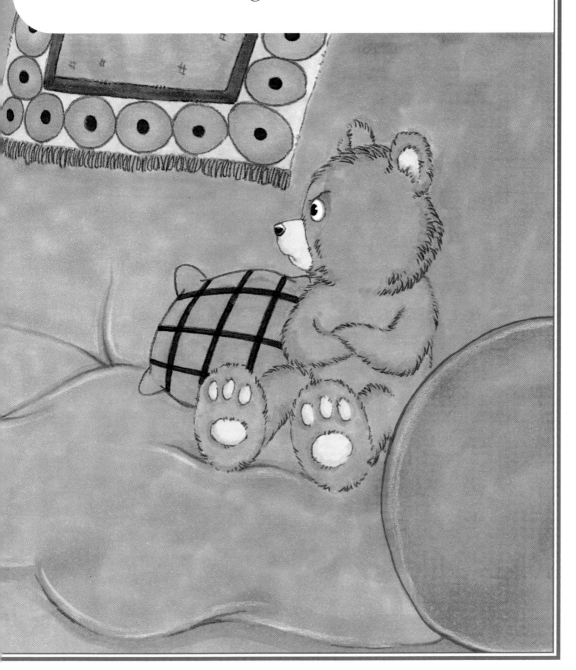

As the cubs sat staring at each other, two raccoons drove by. Seeing that the door was open, they stopped and peeked inside. "Hello," they called. "Is anyone home?"

Neither Stubby nor Prissy spoke or moved.

"It's clear!" whispered one raccoon. "I don't see anyone except two stuffed teddy bears."

They walked in and went straight to work. One raccoon headed for the kitchen and emptied all the shelves of dishes and food. The other removed everything from the bedroom.

"Is Stubby so foolish as to sit there and let those raccoons steal all our things?" thought Prissy.

Stubby never moved or said a word.

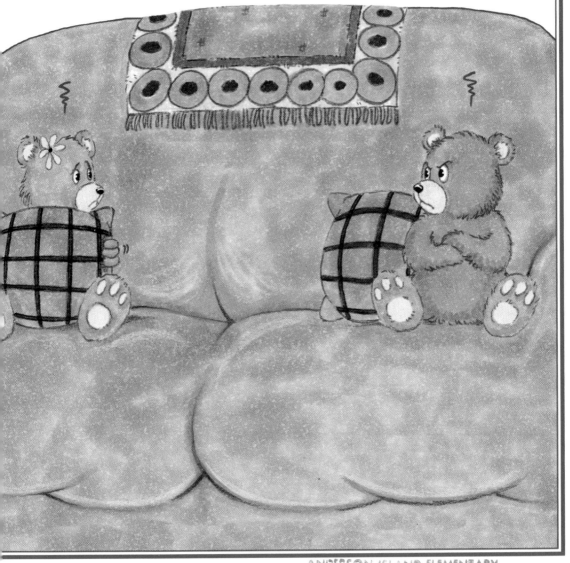

Stubby watched as one raccoon took Mama's purse. Stubby was so mad that he almost yelled at Prissy. Instead, he grumbled to himself, "I can't believe stubborn Prissy is going to let that raccoon steal Mama's purse. Mama is so close, but she won't even call her!"

The cubs quietly watched the raccoons remove every last item from the house, except the couch they sat on.

"Quick!" said one of the bandits. "Let's get out of here."

In a flash, they left the house and sped away in their loaded-down truck.

Prissy could not believe what had happened. "That stubborn Stubby let them steal my bed, my pretty clothes, and even my new doll!"

But she held back her tears and vowed, "I'll never give in!"

Stubby was so angry his insides began to shake.

"She did it!" he fumed. "She let them steal everything—our food, our furniture, Mama's purse—even my favorite ball glove!"

Just then the cubs heard a loud scream. Outside their door a hungry wolf was chasing a little lost kitten.

"Help! Help!" cried the baby kitty. "Please, somebody help me!"

The wolf sneered, "I'm hungry, and I'm going

to eat you!"

No one moved inside the house.

As the wolf drew closer, the scared little kitten closed her eyes and screamed as loudly as she could. "Help me! Please! Somebody—please help me!"

The wolf opened his jaws wide and was just
about to swallow his dinner, when...Wham!!! A
bear claw smacked him on the side of his head,
hurling him against a tree.

The scared wolf did not know what hit him. He shook his head, sprung to his feet, and ran as fast as he could back into the forest.

The kitten opened her eyes and smiled at the bear who had saved her life. It was Prissy. She had run out of the house to save the kitten.

Then Prissy and the kitten heard a loud clapping sound. It was Stubby. He was jumping up and down, clapping his hands and shouting, "I won! I won!"

Then with a great big smile Stubby yelled, "Remember, Prissy? You move, you lose! Come now and shut the door!"

Prissy and the baby kitten stared at Stubby.

"How could he care only about winning?" wondered Prissy.

When Stubby saw the scared little kitten, he stopped clapping and his smile disappeared.

Just then the cubs saw Papa and Mama coming with a box filled with berries and nuts.

"Oh no!" moaned Stubby as he remembered the empty house. "What's Papa going to say?"

"We're in big, big trouble," said Prissy.

Stubby and Prissy were scared.

As Papa and Mama walked up, Stubby tried to explain, "It's all my fault. I've been very foolish."

"I'm as much to blame as Stubby," said Prissy with a shaky voice. "I was just as foolish and stubborn."

Papa and Mama never said a word. They slowly walked to the door and looked inside.

"What happened?" asked Mama.

Stubby began to cry. "I'm sorry, Mama. It's all my fault."

Prissy wiped her eyes. "We were foolish. We let some raccoons come into our house and steal everything."

Papa put his arms around Stubby and Prissy and asked, "Why did you—"

Just as Papa was speaking, a truck pulled up
loaded with food, dishes, and furniture.

"Get them, Papa!" shouted Stubby. "They're
the ones who stole all our things!"

"Yes!" yelled Prissy. "They're the ones!"

Just then the forest friends came and began unloading the truck. First the dishes, then the food, and then the furniture—everything was brought back.

Then one of the raccoons handed Mama her purse and Prissy her doll. The other one handed Stubby his ball glove.

"Was all this a joke?" asked Stubby.

"Well," explained Ricky Rabbit, "we saw you and Prissy sitting on the couch and acting stubborn. So we asked the raccoons to do something to show you how silly it is to act that way."

The raccoons added, "We told your dad and mom about it when they were picking berries. We hope you're not mad."

"I'm not mad," said Prissy.

"Neither am I," agreed Stubby. "We learned an important lesson."

Now everyone laughed about what had happened.

"Thank you for helping us learn how foolish it is to be proud and stubborn," said Prissy.

Stubby looked around and noticed someone was missing. "Where's the wolf?" he asked.

The forest friends were scared. "What wolf?"

"You know," said Stubby, "that mean looking wolf that chased the baby kitten."

The forest friends were puzzled.

"We didn't send a wolf," said Bucky Beaver.

Stubby looked at Prissy and said, "Then you really did save the little baby kitten."

"You're a hero!" said Ricky Rabbit.

All the forest friends clapped their hands and shouted, "Prissy is a hero! Hooray!!!"

Stubby walked over to Prissy and said, "Prissy, you moved—but you sure didn't lose."

One by one the forest friends left. Then Papa, Mama, Stubby, and Prissy went into their house.

"What a day!" said Papa as he sat down to relax. "What a day!"

Then Papa noticed that the front door was open. "Would someone please close the door for me?" he asked.

With a bounce, two young cubs raced to the door. Yes, Stubby and Prissy had learned their lesson.